For Olivia & Levi

Night Time Animals

Written & Illustrated by
Andy Hart

In the valley, by light of the moon,
Comes a mother and baby raccoon.

A wolf sits by and gives out a howl
While from the trees swoops a great horned owl.

The glow from the fire flies is really awesome.
So is the playful group of opossums.

The bats fly up to a moonlit sky
As wild cats watch with big glowing eyes.

A whip-poor-will sings from a large weeping willow.
Then out of the ground comes a fat armadillo.

The crickets in the grass like to hop & chirp.
Listen to the frogs as they ribbit & burp.

A bumpy brown toad sits under some rocks
While over the hill comes a dashing red fox.

All through the night the animals play.
Then the sun rises at the break of day.

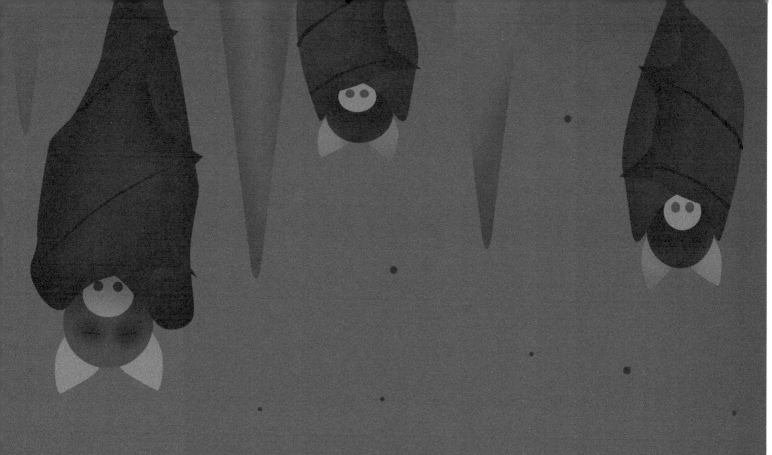

They go to their beds and curl up real tight
And stay there and sleep until the next night.

The End